The Newsroom

The Newsroom

A Novella

David Osborn

DAGMAR
MIURA
LOS ANGELES

Published by Dagmar Miura
Los Angeles
www.dagmarmiura.com

The Newsroom

Copyright © 2024 David Osborn
All rights reserved. No part of this book may be used or reproduced in any manner whatsoever without prior written permission except in the case of brief quotations embodied in critical articles or reviews. For information, address Dagmar Miura, dagmarmiura@gmail.com, or visit our website at www.dagmarmiura.com.

This is a work of fiction. Names, characters, businesses, places, events, and incidents are either the products of the author's imagination or used in a fictitious manner. Any resemblance to actual persons, living or dead, or actual events is purely coincidental.

First published 2024

ISBN: 979-8-89195-038-2

For Robin

One

"Three. Hey there, Three! Hello."

The demanding cry for one of his seven children by Sean Kaitland, whom more often than not he quirkily identified by number, echoed through his rather ramshackle house in the suburbs of the small city of Farmingdale. Sean, a normally self-controlled topography surveyor, stood in the hallway with his transit ready to go to work in his job, which currently was changing the contour lines around the city's new reservoir. About to leave, he had become aware that he didn't have his smaller equipment bag with its GPS system, which he felt sure he might need for the job that day. He had been explaining the system to his daughter Clarity after dinner the night before as Clarity, his third child in a row, was always curious, and among all his children seemed the most interested and able to understand the nature of his job.

"Three," he cried again, and almost at the same time his call was answered by his daughter's appearance.

"Dad? What?"

Clarity, in some ways Sean's favorite child and one who was always special to his conservative eccentricities and even more tolerant of his forgetfulness than Angel, his ever patient wife and children's mother, was a young woman barely twenty, who had just finished a year in community college and was looking for a job.

Not considered particularly pretty in any classical sense, Clarity had an earnest expression of curiosity in a face which, beneath her crown of black curly hair that covered her forehead nearly to her eyebrows and fell down the sides of her head to her neck, some considered nerdy, and perhaps indeed she was a bit of a nerd.

A basically shy person who was almost reclusive and had little if anything in common with her peers at school, many of whom shunned her as an oddball or just plain weird, she cared little for the likes and habits of most young women her age. She disdained makeup, pop music with all its super glamorized singers, as well as NFL football and NBA basketball heroes, and was more often seen with her nose in a book than not. She was currently reading up on early pre-Athenian poetry in ancient Greek history.

Yet with all that which could only be considered a big minus among those of her age, there was something about her that was endearing. Perhaps it was simply her earnestness or the intensity of her look when something of real interest struck her fancy. Perhaps it was her down-to-earth quality. Whatever it was, and while marking her different from most, at the same time it marked her as more interesting to a certain level of people with serious intellect.

That was all the plus in her character. The minus was that, unlike her father and mother both, and especially her father, she never took a positive stance on any current issues that were controversial or espoused any causes demanding support. She thought little about politics, which seemed to her to inflame most people, as it did her father, and which she chose not to understand at all. When the TV news came on at six o'clock, mostly on Fox, and blared away in the daytime during weekends when she wasn't at school, she invariably switched channels to ESPN or CSPN sports, her favorite being, so contrary to her physical appearance, of all things, rugby.

"What, Dad?" Clarity repeated.

"My GPS. The blue bag."

"You left it on the kitchen table, Dad."

"Right. Have a great day." And Sean was gone out the door and off to work with all his equipment to meet an equally hard working soul who was his assistant.

For Clarity it was yet another day of looking for a job and finding herself unqualified for anything in particular, having studied only literature and its historical origins in ancient Greek civilization at community college. Even while still at school, she had begun job hunting and had tried what seemed to her as everywhere while enduring endless refusals because, as her ever practical mother firmly stated, "a study of the humanities gives a person no qualifications for anything in this day and age except more reading."

Frustrated, Clarity kept at it, however, knowing she couldn't give up. To place a classified you had to note previous occupation and, if school, what your studies had been. There was no point in lying; the truth would come out in an interview, so she kept at it. She had to start earning money to add to the family income, with her parents suffering from the rising prices of everything due to inflation, especially groceries and gas for the family car, soon to be past retirement age, and with four children, all at home, and herself included, to feed.

She'd tried Craigslist; she'd even appealed on Instagram and Facebook, all to no avail, and with no success she'd turned to the classifieds in the influential county newspaper, *The Farmingdale Weekly News,* the readership of which extended far beyond its county periphery, influencing many across the politically pivotal state.

"If I were you," Angel said in her usual no-nonsense way, and meaning that's an order, so do it, "I'd hightail it down to the damn newspaper and ask them to list your appeal big, so people would be sure to see it and find it important. Put a frame around it and dark print so it couldn't be missed. What good are they if nobody answers your ad when they always tout their classifieds as the sure way to go for whatever?"

Accordingly, when Clarity had helped Angel wash up the breakfast things, had seen her younger siblings off to school and her two older sisters to work, and had tidied herself up in her best skirt and blouse, she took off for *The Farmingdale Weekly News,* which was housed in an old brick building just off Main Street in downtown Farmingdale.

Two

Farmingdale wasn't a town that had yet grown enough to be called a city but a busy place nevertheless and the capital of important and influential Bosworth County.

In keeping with that influence, *The Farmingdale Weekly News,* with only a staff of thirteen, was seen as an icon by its widespread readership. Led by ageing Elsworth Barnes, an important force in liberal thinking and outlook, its mission was not just to provide people with the kind of local news they couldn't get from either television or big city papers like *The Washington Post* or *The New York Times* but in crusading against a slow inroad into American politics and thinking by the extreme right and its more and, more openly, white nationalism.

When Clarity approached the doors of the paper, her jumble of thoughts were only to protest why nobody answered the ads she'd placed several times in its classified columns. Virtually apolitical, she saw *The Farmingdale Weekly News* as either merely for its classifieds or for whatever local reporting it did on things like auto accidents or the winning basketball scores of the Farmingdale High School team.

Entering, she was greeted by the usual confusing babble of any newsroom from which she was temporarily barred by a counter behind which lurked the imposing figure of a large frizzy-haired blond and bosomy woman who came away from a nearby desk, where she was busy with various stacks of paper, to asked formally, "Yes? May I help you?"

Clarity, a little awed by the unexpected appearance of all the busy people in the newsroom, summoned up her courage and stammered out that she needed to talk to someone in classifieds. In doing so, she inspired an immediate question from the large and imposing woman.

"Is there a problem? I can probably help. I'm Geraldine Banner and I run the classifieds."

The unexpected confrontation with the person in charge of classifieds took Clarity off balance, and it was a moment before she could organize her thinking enough to explain that she had mailed in her availability for a job several times along with the necessary fee and with no success. She couldn't keep spending money without some sort of guarantee of results.

"I'm afraid nobody can give you any such guarantee," the woman said. "When did you advertise?"

Clarity gave her what she thought were the right dates, beginning with the first ad placed three weeks ago, and then waited apprehensively while the classifieds manager, muttering to herself, peered over her large horn-rims first to find a back copy of the paper then to study the fine print of the numerous classifieds that were listed.

When she finally spoke, it was to say, "Is this one yours, and another the week before just like it? Humanities student and so on. Good heavens, child, you wonder why nobody replied? Who on earth cares about the humanities? They're no qualification for a job."

Clarity's voice rose defensively. "What's wrong with my saying I studied the humanities?"

"Nothing at all that I know of." The surprising response came unexpectedly from an elderly man who had heard Clarity's protest just as he was passing behind the classifieds manager. His hair a white cap, he peered at Clarity through old-fashioned spectacles that matched the worn cardigan he wore over a blue work shirt. "What seems to be the problem, Geraldine?" he went on to say, addressing himself to the classifieds woman.

"The young lady's having trouble with her ad," she replied.

"No, I'm not," Clarity said instantly, and rushed on undaunted. "I've placed three with no answers, and I filled in the application correctly, I'm sure."

"She put the same in all three," Geraldine Banner said. "Humanities student seeks full time employment and …"

"What's wrong with that?" came from Clarity in a burst-out interruption, so contrary to her normal nondisputing nature. She had recognized the elderly man as somehow being authority, perhaps even important, and there was an unconscious call for help in her voice.

"Let's have a look," he said, coming to the counter where the pages carrying the classified ads were spread out.

"I thought maybe to work in the library or a book store someplace," Clarity said as he looked down at the ads. "Is this the one, Geraldine?" he asked.

"Yes, sir, Mr. Barnes." Geraldine pointed the offending ad out to him.

There was a moment's silence broken only by the elderly man saying, "Hmm …" and "Ah …" until he finally looked up from the ad at Clarity. "And you are who?"

It was a demand to be answered, and Clarity found herself saying, "My name's Clarity Kaitland," and nothing more, and waiting expectantly.

"Hmm," the old man said again. "Kaitland?" And then, "Sean Kaitland's daughter?"

"Yes, sir," came from Clarity, whose surprise was echoed by the expression on the face of the classifieds manager.

"County surveyor," the old man explained to the less than sympathetic Geraldine. "Good man other than his far-right politics. Known him off and on for years. Has a raft of kids he quaintly numbers, as I remember." And then to Clarity, "What number are you, young lady?"

"I'm Three, sir," Clarity found herself saying in awed surprise.

"I'm Elsworth Barnes, Miss Kaitland," the old man said. "Come with me." He turned to Geraldine as he went, saying, "I've got this one," and after waving for Clarity to follow, heading off through the newsroom.

"Mr. Barnes is the paper's senior editor," a clearly respectful Geraldine said when, rather numbed with surprise and not knowing what to expect, Clarity came obediently around the counter to follow the venerable editor through all the confusion of the newsroom while uncomfortably aware of the stares she was getting from everyone before going into a small office, clearly the domain of the editor and separated from all the reporters and writers by a glass-paned door and windows.

Clarity had hardly obeyed Elsworth Barnes's order to take a seat when he said, "Humanities, eh? Just what in the humanities?"

A bewildered Clarity stumbled a reply. "Mostly early Greek, sir. Pre-Homeric poetry. What is known about the Mycenean bards before Homer and …"

She didn't get to say more. Barnes interrupted.

"Good, good. The Greeks are most important in anyone's education. And not enough of it for youngsters today." Then, "Are you familiar with the SPLC?"

Clarity's thinking came to an abrupt halt. "Sir?"

"The Southern Poverty Law Center. I want to know their findings on the Liberty Boys, that crowd of crazies just started up out in Oklahoma, of course, where else. When last heard the SPLC was in hot pursuit.".

With that Barnes picked up a landline phone and began making a call, abruptly dismissing her but throwing an aside to Geraldine Banner, who had followed and stood hesitating in the doorway, seconds before his call was answered, "Find her a corner someplace, Geraldine. Marie's, or whatever her name, when she was still with us."

Not knowing quite what she felt, Clarity found herself led by a now pleasantly smiling and noticeably more friendly Geraldine through the busy newsroom to an alcove that was not much more than an open closet, and on the way meeting a number of the newspaper's employees: a tall, lanky, dark-haired, and rather severe Roslind Bernstein, the managing editor; Alter Maulen, a scholarly intense copy editor; Newsome Barret, a columnist; and Randy Colefield and Sally Sommersville, both writers.

Only when seated at a desk with a PC monitor and keyboard did it finally sink in to Clarity that she had a job, and not only a job, but one with the prestigious *Farmingdale Weekly News,* under the direction of its famous editor Elsworth Barnes, who she learned to her astonishment was an enthusiastic reader of Greek history when he wasn't using the newspaper to espouse liberal causes.

Three

Coming home after her first day at *The Farmingdale Weekly News,* Clarity wasn't quite greeted by the reception she expected. Instead of a babble of happy congratulations from her mother, Angel, and siblings, Abigail and Arlene, numbered one and two, there was an immediate cautious questioning, especially from her father.

"You've got hired by that newspaper itself?" Her father's brow was furrowed with immediate worry. "I thought you were just going to use their classifieds."

Angel quickly said, "What your father means, Clarity, is that *The Farmingdale Weekly News* is terribly controversial."

"Exactly," Sean said. "Anyone who works for

them could find themselves in trouble. And we don't want any reaction to them, especially to that editor fellow Barnes, spilling over into our family. I've worked too hard to have trouble at work."

It was a direct counterpoint to the weeks of silence that had previously greeted Clarity's every failed attempt to find work. That morning, when firmly ensconced at the desk in the alcove corner of the busy newsroom assigned to her by the undaunted Geraldine, she had dared to sneak in a phone call to her mother.

"And guess what, Mom," she'd whispered after warily casting an eye about to make sure she wasn't heard. "Mr. Barnes likes early pre-Homeric poetry in Corinth and Syracuse too."

There'd been a long moment's silence before Clarity heard her mother say, "Clarity, be careful. Surely he didn't hire you to study the Greeks."

"No, Mom," Clarity said. "He has me swatting up on the SPLC."

"The what?"

"The Southern Poverty Law Center. They're experts on hate groups."

Another silence before her mother said, "Tell us all about it at dinner," before hanging up.

It was again the same when she got home. Sean Kaitland quite openly objected to her working for people who he said could cause him and the family trouble. Sean was an ardent supporter of the presidential hopeful, Tory Lundt, who, along with all his followers, espoused as the truth endless conspiracy theories and wore a cap emblazoned with the words "America for God."

The Farmingdale Weekly News was openly opposed to both Lundt and his party. "I've heard of your SPLC and I don't like it," Sean said when the SPLC came up at dinner. "They're trouble, and newspapers should stick to the news and not support them."

Even though clearly hired and a member of the influential newspaper, Clarity tried not to let her parent's surprising disapproval follow her to work. Settling in, and in spite of crossing swords with the frosty no-nonsense, all-work managing editor, Roslind Bernstein, who didn't bother to hide a different attitude toward her than Barnes, she met several of the more important members of the newspaper's staff. There was friendly Tracy Tangerton, a pleasantly talkative city hall politics reporter who stopped at her desk to welcome her, and she met a whimsical little guy named Arnold Capeheart who reported on crime and who, out of curiosity, came to her alcove desk full of questions—who was she, where had she previously worked?

In spite of her family's open suspicion of the newspaper, she quickly felt at home in the busy atmosphere of the newsroom and pride whenever she saw a printed copy of *The Farmingdale Weekly News.* Working for the paper gave her a sense of importance and authority she'd never felt before because the paper was almost always one jump ahead in knowing what was going on than her or her family.

Filled with the energy and determination in a job that she felt somehow placed her above classmates at school and community college who had made no secret of seeing her interest in the humanities as useless, Clarity threw herself into learning everything possible about the wave of hate groups that seemed to have seized every corner of the country.

She was a born researcher, and when twice summoned by the venerable Elsworth Barnes and pumped as to the current extent of the SPLC's investigation into white nationalists or antigovernment hate groups, she found among the vast network of them one the SPLC hadn't got to. It was a neo-Nazi group in the neighboring town of Indian River named Women Warriors. Composed entirely of women, it extolled, in a particularly nasty way, endless false facts and conspiracy theories while idolizing Hitler and Nazism.

Nothing daunted, since they were so close by, Clarity decided on the Fourth of July, when the newspaper was closed for the day, to have a look, and got in her car, and drove to Indian River, hoping if the Women Warriors didn't parade to at least get a sight of some of them, dressed, in her imagination, in the brown uniforms of the female World War II Nazi SS Storm Troopers, notoriously more dangerously cruel than their male counterparts, and carrying swastika banners.

But in the town's swirl of celebrations, she found and saw nothing of the Women Warriors themselves, and came away with only a few souvenirs to indicate their existence. It was almost as though the group, she realized, like many hate cults, wasn't there. Along with hundreds of others all across the country, they only emerged to proclaim their presence when exposed publicly or when they felt it safe to do so.

When Clarity told Elsworth Barnes what she'd done, the venerable old editor acted as expected. "So close by?" And then, "Damnable hate groups. We've been too silent too long about them." He called out to his managing editor, Roslind Bernstein. "Roslind, have you heard of this Indian River bunch our young Kaitland has unearthed? And can you believe it, right next door at Indian River?"

"No, sir," Roslind replied. And added, in a rather icy criticism of Clarity, "Miss Kaitland hasn't seen to share her information with me."

Her senior editor ignored her, and he was quick and short with his order. "When you lay out for next week, leave space on the front page. It's about time I wrote an editorial about all these the groups everywhere that are plaguing our nation."

Four

Roslind Bernstein dutifully followed orders, and the front page of *The Farmingdale Weekly News* the next week was emblazoned with the following headlined editorial.

Recent events have brought this newspaper to take a harder look than ever at the extraordinary rage that seems to be sweeping every corner of our nation. Fed by the conspiracy theories that defy imagination and have the current president guilty of everything from sexual assault to outright murder as well as at the will of foreign governments, the angry unrest spurred on by a would-be occupant of the White House is seen everywhere, not just in Washington but in every small town and village, in every farm and city dwelling, while fanned into flames by endless lies and fabrications passed off as truth.

This newspaper has a serious question to ask its

readers. Why are we doing this to ourselves? Why are we following forces of evil like the children who followed the Pied Piper of Hamlin? Why are we turning our backs on what we stand for, when from our earliest years at home and at school we are taught never to lie, that bullying and deceit are wrong, to respect rules and laws, and ultimately to hold in profound respect the judgment of the now regrettably corrupt United States Supreme Court. Why are we substituting hate and adversity, spread endlessly abroad in conspiracy theories and lies and the utter distortion of fact, by a narcissistic psychopath to replace what in our hearts we seems to have forgotten is right?

Our country is awash with over two hundred hate groups claiming patriotism. It should and must be the task of every single one of us to root them out in a public pledge before they achieve their mindless aims of destruction. Following are a few nearby.

The paper then listed a dozen hate groups selected from the those named by the SPLC, among them the Women Warriors that Clarity had unearthed close by, and the reaction by readers was gratifying. A hundred supporting letters poured in, among them a pamphlet one reader had received that showed a group of women in storm-trooper brown shirts with swastika armbands giving a Heil Hitler salute to a leader. Clarity found it her job to briefly respond to each with the newspaper's thanks.

The reaction at home, however, was what might have been expected. Sean Kaitland was at once fearful for his job, and with his wife, Angel, joining in, wasted no time in expressing his fears.

Seated at the kitchen table with wife and family,

Sean said to Clarity, "I for one am most certainly not writing in any pledge to do anything, number Three. I've held down my job for over thirty years now by keeping my mouth shut and my opinions to myself about any and everything that was even remotely controversial. You are where you are today, young lady, still living in the comfortable and safe home in which you were raised because of me, and don't forget it. You should quit this job of yours, where you risk embarrassing yourself and your entire family with you, and look for employment elsewhere."

Clarity tried to fight back. "But Dad, it's exactly people like us that Mr. Barnes is appealing to. The hate is everywhere. Don't you remember on television that riot in Charlottesville, when a whole crowd of men marched with flaming torches chanting, 'Jews shall not replace us.'"

"They were a handful of nutcases and soon forgotten."

"Dad, they were a lot more than a handful."

Her mother broke in. "Clarity, enough. Your newspaper talks big about everyone like us being led around by the nose, but it's doing the same thing with its preaching to ordinary working people, and making us look in the wrong somehow."

"Mom, the SPLC …" Clarity wanted to point out that the newspaper got its authority about the wave of national hate groups from an outfit whose information was universally respected, but she was cut short by her father, who banged the table angrily.

"Enough, Three. I heard about them. Bunch of commies or close to it. One of the guys at work said, and if you ask me, hell bent on stirring up trouble for some damn reason and nothing else. They're just as bad as the people they claim are dangerous."

Sean's outbursts put an end to further talk, and Clarity was left feeling deeply wounded and torn between two lives. One, her life at work, which had come to mean so much to her; the other, her life at home. For the first time ever, she was faced with a strident difference in the truth between herself and her parents and a raw realization that both her mother and father, long her guiding icons, were exactly the people to whom her editor Elsworth Barnes was appealing.

Vainly, she tried to find a way to weather the storm her father's outburst created in her. Silence and a mumbled acquiescence brought momentary peace to the dinner table, and she guiltily avoided her father at breakfast the following morn.

But at work, it was gratefully different. Discomfort at home was replaced with an intense feeling of pride in the newspaper and joy when at her desk. When she explained the dilemma she felt herself in to Benny Cranz, a writer with whom she'd become friendly, sharing with him as she had with Elsworth Barnes her love of ancient history, his immediate suggestion was, "Why don't you show them the pamphlet you collected on that Heil Hitler bunch over at Indian River? What's their name—the Women Warriors? And news reports about some other hate group marching last year up at the state capitol."

Benny was right, Clarity thought. Her father was going to have to believe in hate menace when he saw the Nazi pamphlet, and she planned to find an auspicious moment to corner her father with it.

She never got the chance. Others besides her parents would take issue with Elsworth Barnes front page editorial, and far more seriously.

Five

Friday, two weeks later, and a busy day for *The Farmingdale Weekly News*. Late Thursday night there'd been a derailment of a freight train some distance from Farmingdale on the rail line that ran right by the town, cutting through its outskirts and providing a station for commuters who worked an hour away in distant Three City Junction.

The newspaper's principal reporters, Tracy Tangerton and Alex Devers, were at the scene of the derailment, leaving Arnold Capeheart and Sally Sommersville to cover any other news, Arnold news in general and Sally on anything local.

Elsworth Barnes was at his desk pondering another editorial for the following week's paper.

His managing editor, steely Roslind Bernstein, was discussing a column by the paper's opinion writer, Newsome Barret. Frizzy-haired Geraldine Banner was at her usual post behind the classified counter.

Checking on ads placed the day before, Geraldine was the first to meet the incoming woman who, dressed in a dark hooded sweat suit, was carrying an AR-15 fitted with a bump stock and capable of firing a thousand rounds of death a minute.

"Good morning," Geraldine said automatically and as usual without even looking up. "Can I help you?"

They were her last words before a quick burst of shots took her down, half her head blown away by one, several others tearing into her body, leaving blood, skull fragments, and frizzy hair spattered everywhere.

Done with her, the woman calmly pushed her way past the classified counter and without hesitation sprayed the room with bursts of automatic rifle fire that brought instant death to Sally Sommersville and Arnold Capeheart before they could move, and even as they registered astonished fear.

Ignoring wounded Roslind Bernstein, who lay only half conscious on the floor suffering shots to her head, body, and legs, the woman went straight to the glass-enclosed office of Elsworth Barnes, who in a sudden uncomprehending moment of shock had risen from his desk to see the woman's rapid approach through the bloody chaos of bodies and overturned desks she had created.

"Good morning, Mr. Barnes," the woman said with icy calmness that was almost a monotone, and smiling, at the same time fingering the trigger of the AR-15.

A moment's awful silence, and as fast as she'd come, the woman was gone, leaving four dead and two dying, Alter Maulen, the copy editor, and Newsome Barret, op-ed columnist, whose lives were fast fading away in unchecked bleeding.

And Clarity? Where was she?

Half hidden at her desk in the semi-alcove and caught completely off guard, she had looked up, startled and uncomprehending, at the sudden blast of shots, only to see Geraldine crash down to the floor a bloody mess, and her killer step silently around the counter, AR-15 raised again to immediately begin spraying the room with death.

Her thinking stopped, Clarity sat frozen in a blank stare even as Elsworth Barnes rose from his desk, hands instinctively raised in useless protection. She saw but didn't see. The rain of death that swept the newsroom so instantly and left her unable to do more than blankly register the fallen bodies, the overturned chairs and shattered desks. Frozen in what her eyes took in, her brain failed to understand. She saw the rapid strides of the woman killer as she finished her deadly attack and left the room, but she stood frozen, shock-numb in every part of her body, still staring blindly and not registering.

The terrible silence that followed was finally broken by a far distant sound of a siren. Someone upstairs in the building, or next door, heard the shots, and recognizing them as not being firecrackers but from an automatic rifle, had heart-in-mouth hurriedly dialed 911.

A cautious and half-frightened police officer, Glock raised, was the first to enter the newsroom. Another officer followed, both protectively looking for who had fired the shots even as they took in the room's deathly chaos. One saw Clarity. His gun swung around on her. He screamed out, "You. Don't move. Hands on your head."

She didn't move. Couldn't. Nor could she speak in answer to his repeated shouts of, "Hands on head, hands on head." She couldn't hear him as, gun pointed, he rushed on her with impulsive panicked speed to seize her, spin her around and slam her to the ground, arms roughly twisted behind her back and handcuffs out.

A paramedic coming into the room saved her from further police error. "Hey, slow down, man. She's in shock. Can't you see? In shock. Uncuff her. We'll take over."

In a blurred confusion of voices, Clarity later was to remember being gently walked out of the newsroom onto the street, seeing the many more police everywhere, and the police cars, and the waiting ambulances. She remembered being laid down on a stretcher, someone in uniform giving her a shot, the rumble of movement and low sound as the ambulance drove away. And its siren somewhere very close by but muffled.

She remembered a sudden glare of bright light in a hospital ER, voices all around, a nurse then a doctor and herself covered with a blanket, and then finally registering all she had witnessed. And then nothing more.

Six

News of the worst mass shooting in the state's history quickly became national, and the media from everywhere descended on Farmingdale: television, radio, the press. Six members of *The Farmingdale Weekly News* were dead. Those of the staff who were alive, though injured, were quickly cornered at the hospital to be endlessly interviewed with little to report.

They were a badly wounded Roslind Bernstein and news writer Benny Cranz, both with leg and torso wounds, and two others, writer Betsy Brine, hit in the stomach just as she had risen from her desk to refill her coffee, and reporter Randy Colefield.

None could remember much if anything at all

of the slaughter other than the sudden appearance of a strange hooded woman along with the immediate and near deafening repetitive explosive roar of shots. It had all happened machine-gun quickly.

So Clarity, for the most part recovered and accompanied by the Farmingdale police chief and the state's attorney general, who had taken over the investigation, became the principal target, her stunned family with her, of all the media, from television's CNN to *The Washington Post* and *The New York Times.*

Their house besieged, Sean Kaitland and his wife, Angel, somehow managed to find a few words to say that their daughter was okay before firmly refusing to speak further and leaving Clarity as the sole unhurt witness to the shooting to face an army of reporters alone.

"Did you see who it was?" "Was there more than one?" "Did they fire at random or on individuals?" "Did they say anything?" "Why were you spared?"

And threaded endlessly throughout all their questioning, demands to know how long she'd worked for the newspaper, what her position there was, what her thoughts about the shooting were, had she been close to Elsworth Barnes or particularly close to anyone else?

And of course endless questions about her home life, her friends, her years at high school. Nothing was spared, including her interest in the pre-Homeric bards in ancient Greek history, which instantly aroused interest in Greek historians, who at once bombarded the Kaitland mailbox.

One of these came out of the blue and as a complete surprise, first in the form of a man who had passed through several local police posted by the town as protection for the family. He flashed a badge that said he was U.S. Secret Service with a message from the President of the United States and to an astonished Clarity, who had answered the door, held out a cell phone.

"The President is on speaker phone," the agent said, and Clarity, almost dumbstruck with surprise, heard the President say how glad he was that she had survived such a terrible ordeal, and after encouraging words and a wish for a quick recovery, signed off with a chuckle and the remark that Clarity was ahead of him in her early pre-Homeric Greek history. "I only got as far back as the Trojan Wars," he said before hanging up.

Somebody got hold of the remark and leaked it to the press, and Clarity found herself the center of yet further uproar. Pictures of her wearing the big black-rimmed glasses that almost hid her scholarly face, shyly peering out at the world through a mass of tiny black curls, were seen everywhere.

Meanwhile, what of Clarity's parents? Sean Kaitland and his wife, Angel, hardly dared venture from home without being accosted, and thought it would never end. Especially irritating, almost frightening, was a visit from two top executives of the SPLC, who spent an hour with Clarity questioning her about her interest in the Women Warriors that they had not yet registered. Sean Kaitland found it hard to accept that the organization he'd so disparaged was not only clearly legitimate, if not more so, but had actually come to his home. He and his wife loved their famous daughter, but both ardently wished she'd never gone to work for *The Farmingdale Weekly News,* and prayed for it all to end.

And it finally did, with only one more surprise to come. Sean Kaitland had taken the family landline receiver off its hook from the day of the massacre to avoid it endlessly ringing, and Clarity, alone in the house with both parents back at work, thought to call a friend, and dared to put the receiver back up. She'd hardly done so when it rang. Fearfully, she answered and prepared to hang up instantly.

"Hello?"

"Is this Clarity?"

Something told Clarity not to hang up. The voice didn't sound like the usual curious. It sounded weak, almost feeble, and very hesitant, as though the caller had trouble speaking.

"Clarity, this is Roslind Bernstein. When would you feel like coming back to work?"

Seven

"Number Three, have you completely lost your mind? I don't care if some fool is thinking to start the paper up again. You are not going back to that place, and no arguments." That was Sean Kaitland.

"Dad's right, Clarity." That was Sean's wife, Angel.

Clarity was badly taken aback by their immediate anger the moment she'd announced Bernstein's call, and tried to protest. "Dad, Mom. What's wrong with going back to work? I need a job."

"Yes, you do, but not with that damned newspaper. Have you thought even one moment how our whole family would be inundated by the press all over again?"

"Who's this Bernstein woman, anyway, Three?"

"She's the managing editor, Dad."

"Managing editor of what?" Her father demanded. "By all reports the place was left a shambles, and half the newspeople there killed."

Angel sniffed. "Make sense, Clarity. Find a job somewhere else. I'll see if there isn't a place down at the supermarket. They're always short someone or other. Maybe back in the stockroom."

It was that way the whole day, until something along with a natural stubborn streak in Clarity took over, an unusual surge of something she was at loss to identify, but was loyalty—an intense surge of it. Not to her parents, but for the first time ever, to something far from them. It was loyalty to the job that had been hers at *The Farmingdale Weekly News* and to Elsworth Barnes, who had believed in her.

By nightfall the feeling had increased, and she lapsed into a stubborn silence, torn between her parents' objections and her love for them and a deep-seated nagging desire to do something she wanted to do, even if it was so far out of the ordinary and even to herself seemed a little crazy. Trying to sleep, she was tormented by a constantly returning memory of Elsworth Barnes behind the counter with frizzy-haired Geraldine when he'd asked, "The Greeks are most important in anyone's education. And not enough of it for youngsters today." And telling Geraldine to find her a desk someplace, perhaps Marie's, who had departed.

And sleepless, remembering the rush of emotion

she'd felt hearing him say that, and then the awful memory of seeing him raise his hands protectively before the fusillade of AR-15 shots, his white hair and tired face, his glasses flying, his mouth open in a useless shout, and his falling.

In the morning, she maintained a seeming compliant silence when both parents went off to work, her father to his surveying, her mother to the supermarket. Then when she was assured of no interference and the further emotionalism of divided loyalties, she left the house and made her way across town to the offices of *The Farmingdale Weekly News.*

From the outside the place looked the same, the same gold letters across the broad glass besides the entrance door. The same except that everything around, the street, the rest of the old brick building, all seemed stifled into a kind of deathly silence.

A little frightened, Clarity reached for the door handle. The door yielded, and she cautiously pushed it open, and then, heart in mouth, stepped inside to find herself in the newsroom.

Nothing looked the same. And yet it did. There were all the same desks she remembered from before, although some were missing where Sally Sommersville and Newsome Barret had sat, and Clarity felt she could almost still see them, bent over and peering intently into their laptops.

And where was big, bosomy, frizzy-haired Geraldine Banner? The reception counter where she had always stood, dominating, was eerily empty.

Clarity had a brief flickering image of Geraldine in her mind as a different and ugly form, spinning away from the counter and downward.

For a moment, when time seemed to stand still, and Clarity once again heard the insistent and deadly popping roar of the AR-15, a deathly silence was broken by the slightly quavering voice of the once icy Roslind Bernstein.

"Clarity, you came. I'm so glad. We're rushing to get out next week's edition. It will be much smaller, but a start. Take Newsome Barret's desk there and write his weekly column. I'm sure you can manage."

The once managing editor looked different. Her hair had turned white. She seemed smaller, less a dominating figure, one arm still in a hospital sling and a large padded bandage across one side of her head. "You'll maybe not recognize Tracy Tangerton and Alex Devers. They were both away when it all happened."

Clarity noticed both men for the first time. One, Alex Devers, seemed young like herself, a stocky boyish man with a blond crew cut, and Tracy Tangerton older, beginning to show gray at the temples, and with a slumped figure that went with his rimless glasses.

Another voice broke the murmured silence as both Tangerton and Devers acknowledged her presence. It was Benny Cranz, with whom she had once started a friendship, before he'd been brought down in the hail of death. His torso swathed in bandages, his head also so that he was nearly unrecognizable, he echoed the others in a welcome a bit more personal, since she and he had often spent time chatting and finding things about work and life they shared in common.

Now she heard him say, "Welcome as our new weekly columnist, Clarity. Write a good one for us. Two hundred and fifty words is all poor Newsome used to do. But best get to it because Roslind wants to put the paper to bed tomorrow. A limited edition the first time, but at least getting us all started again."

Clarity felt a flood of emotional warmth toward him at his welcome, and for want of anything else to say, and not wanting to make any observation as to his condition, managed, "Thank you, Benny. Will do my best," before staring down at Newsome Barret's laptop. She turned it on. He had started a column, but only a few words, before the explosion of high-caliber bullets had put an abrupt end to any more. He'd written, "I'd like to talk this week about what our newspaper means to people. Without it, most of us, in fact all of us, live in a sort of blank unknowingness about happenings around us."

Clarity stared silently at the words that stared silently back at her, challenging. Then, hesitantly at first, she wrote, "This newspaper tells people everything going on in Farmingdale; we report on who won the high school football game, us or Wiltonville; we report on accidents and arrests; we let everyone know about the latest from the Ladies

Reading Club; we tell everyone who died and who had just been born and about a new medical clinic. We provide an always busy classified section. We're local and proud of it."

Clarity sat back and looked at what she'd written. Not too bad, she thought. It was a beginning, and she continued to type, "We are Farmingdale's eyes and ears and tell everyone what's going on, not just in Farmingdale but often in the whole county around us. We are something essential to people's lives, a local newspaper."

Eight

It was the first of half a dozen columns she wrote, one a week. Roslind Bernstein ungrudgingly approved each one, and even posted Clarity's latest on the front page. It was one in which Clarity criticized the lies of the flamboyant politician and presidential hopeful Tory Lundt, who forever weighed in against any and every legislation that sought to improve education or general welfare.

Benny Cranz was liberal in his appraisals. "Shades of old Elsworth Barnes," Benny said. Alex Devers and Tracy Tangerton, the two reporters who had been away at the time of the shooting, agreed.

Life slowly returned to *The Farmingdale Weekly News* as Benny and Bernstein, both still struggling to recover from injuries, managed in long hours of overtime work to almost singlehandedly get the various other sections of the newspaper back up to form.

Bernstein had hired a new copy editor, Darcy Evans, to replace Alter Maulen and a writer, Bill Petrovsky, to replace Sally Sommersville. Although severely limited in scope and output, and failing twice to meet deadlines, the Farmingdale weekly was beginning to look its old self.

Clarity, after a first few days of uncertainty, soon settled in to the job. In two months of writing her column, laborious and uncertain work at first, then becoming easier and easier, she began to feel as though she had always worked in journalism, with every aspect of putting a weekly local paper together and to bed as familiar as they were enjoyable, and something she had always done.

There was a good deal more, too, in something she'd never found at school: friendship. She was accepted for thoughts that she no longer felt timid to express, and appreciation for her ability to put those thoughts into printable and readable words to be enjoyed by a host of complete strangers who were the newspapers readers. "Great column this week, Clarity," came more often than not from Roslind Bernstein. And approval from readers came too in letters to the editor.

As she grew into the job, Clarity felt too a new and burgeoning sense of responsibility in being part of something important, and her work at the newspaper a welcome refuge to the very unsimilar reception her efforts received at home.

But it came with a price. At home, a once family happiness with parents and siblings was replaced by an awkward stiffness, as though at times Clarity was a complete stranger. Family routine went about its long accustomed way but with a difference. Silence reigned whenever anything to do with Clarity's work was concerned. Mere mention of *The Farmingdale Weekly News* was strictly off limits.

"Goddamned reactionaries," Sean was heard to mutter if any mention of the newspaper threatened. He had taken to constantly wearing his baseball cap emblazoned with "America for God" to express his loyalty to Tory Lundt, even at dinner.

"Probably deserved what they got," Angel once said unfeelingly about the mindless AR-15 slaughter that had so mercilessly taken the lives of half the newspaper's staff and brought the unwanted onslaught of media to herself and her home, which she felt still burdened with.

Confronted by such a revelation of her parents' politics, which she'd never given a thought to in her school years, Clarity felt all the pain of a division between herself and them. That her parents had joined millions of others who had mindlessly, like the children in "The Pied Piper of Hamlin" or the lemmings following the leader into an ocean death, obediently accepting Jundt's mindless and narcissistic crusade toward autocracy and the destruction of good government, which for hundreds of years had offered an accepted security.

And for the first time in her life, Clarity began to seriously consider leaving her family and finding a home of her own. The shock of what she had witnessed had erased most memories of how she'd lived and felt before the assault. She had made a fresh start and felt determined to stick with it.

"Getting restarted is a hard price we all have had to pay," Benny Cranz said one evening after work, when he and Clarity met at Al's, the local bar frequented by *The Farmingdale Weekly News* staff. "There are several apartments going in my building. Glad to put in a word with the management if you decide to cut the cord."

Clarity, more and more finding herself as wanting to be away from her parents and always being forced to do as they wished, began finally to make up her mind one day, when having a lunch with a girl named Alice, who had been a rare friend at school and now drove an Amazon delivery van.

Living alone in a two-room apartment, Alice was surprised Clarity still lived at home. "Jeepers, Clarity, at least move in with me, if you want, until you find your own place."

Emboldened by Alice, Clarity finally decided one night at dinner, when her father was extolling the virtue of the presidential candidate, Tory Lundt.

"He's a businessman," Sean came out with, ignoring Lundt's history of one bankruptcy after another, "and not one of your starry-eyed liberals who are all talk. He's going to right away, on his first day as President, sort out some of those wishy-washy government departments, like DOJ, or Immigration, that does nothing about millions of rapist criminals pouring over our border every day, and National Security causing problems with Russia."

It was a last straw for Clarity. "The yellow-orange turd is a five times bankrupt loser, Dad," she said, and she announced she was going to live with Alice.

The reaction was as expected. Her mother, Angel, was at once indignant. "Clarity, you will not use language like that in this house." And then, in surprise, when Clarity's announcement sank in, "You're doing what?"

Both of Clarity's older siblings, who still lived at home, remained mute. One worked in the billing department of the phone company, the other supervising at the local laundry mat.

Her father instantly dove into politics and the left-wing stance of *The Farmingdale Weekly News* as misguiding her. "You've been listening too long, Three, to that fool Elsworth Barnes and his nonsense, before, thank God, he was silenced," Sean said. "I knew he'd be trouble the day you went to work there."

Two days later, Clarity waited until both her parents had gone to work, and packing up her few things, silently left for Alice's apartment.

Nine

Roslind Bernstein hurt. All over. Everywhere and constantly. She hurt in both still heavily bandaged legs, where she had received high-caliber bullets. Her head hurt where a bullet had ripped through one cheek, and there was the ceaseless pain where she'd been hit in the chest, causing one lung to collapse, and three shattered ribs repaired.

Why she had lived, the surgeons said, when she was taken by helicopter, unconscious and with nearly fatal loss of blood, to the ER at county hospital, was a medical mystery.

But she did. "One friggin' tough bird," came from one doctor. She lived, and with a nerve and determination that matched her body's fight to survive, got herself back two months after the massacre to the newsroom wreckage of *The Farmingdale Weekly News.*

She was alone there for less than a week, in which she saw phones working again and the return of Benny Cranz, recovering from wounds to his upper body and arms, and Tracy Tangerton and Alex Devers, who had been away the day the woman killer had burst into the newsroom, and, surprisingly, Clarity Kaitland, the massacre's sole witness.

She had also persuaded two more people to join her, Brian Noonan and Agnes Peril, investigative reporters with whom she had once worked when starting a life of journalism at a big city newspaper and who, as with newspaper people countrywide, were profoundly shocked by what had happened and had risen to the defense of getting out the news.

Holding up a copy of the first printing of *The Farmingdale Weekly News,* the visual evidence of all the hard work by everybody in the newsroom, and after congratulating all present, she called out Clarity to speak to personally about Clarity's first effort at writing an op-ed.

"Clarity, this is terrific. It's straight Elsworth Barnes. He'd be so proud of you. I'm going to front-page it next issue. Can you do the next one on Tory Lundt and his America-for-God presidential supporters?"

"I'll try," Clarity said. When Roslind had asked her to assume the op-ed job held by Newsome

Barret, who had died in the fatal fusillade, everything in her had quailed, first at the thought of writing anything, then of daring to fill the shoes of the veteran journalist.

She had said she'd try only because she knew she had somehow to match up to the extraordinary courage and determination of Roslind Bernstein, whom when first working at the newspaper, she had seen as a cold, uncaring, and merciless boss who'd brook no lagging in work by anyone, especially her own self, but who now was a supportive hero who seemed to have complete confidence in her ability live up to Newsome.

"We all have to do jobs we've never done before," Roslind had said when asking Clarity to do the column. "You majored in English. Get with it."

And Clarity had, hesitant at first, but then after her first column extolling the newspaper and its local strength, determined not to let Roslind down. Attacking subjects almost ferociously, she surprised herself with every word she wrote in a burst of defiance of her father, who was always squelching anything she said about anything and forever deprecating the newspaper. She often seized presidential hopeful Tory Lundt as a subject, blatantly referring to him as "the yellow-orange turd" because of his tanning makeup and dyed blond hair, and had castigated his record and his forever wearing, like her father, a bright red baseball hat that announced Lundt's slogan in in bold printed white letters, "America for God."

Today, with Roslind waving the copy of *The Farmingdale Weekly News,* she thought of her father and wondered if ever he would chance to read her op-ed. Probably not, she decided. He didn't subscribe to the paper and get it delivered to his doorstep every morning the way most of his neighbors did.

And just as well, she also thought. Although she had moved from home, she had never wanted the move to be a break in family unity. She still wanted to be "Three" instead of Clarity to her father, which she knew to mean affection, and still valued times she went back home to dinner, in which her job was painfully and carefully avoided, with conversation centered on her mother's supermarket gossip and her father's difficulties with his current surveying.

She had settled in with Alice so well that along with her success in the revival of *The Farmingdale Weekly News,* her small scholarly face, peering out from the cloud of dark curls that framed her whole head while she hunched in silent concentration over her laptop, had become a fixture seen with respect and affection by all, and she felt little need to express her newfound independence.

So, In spite of the brutality of *The Farmingdale Weekly News* massacre, life for Clarity was good. She found living with Alice strange at first, even discomforting, and made certain to keep a distance between herself and Alice to make sharing as easy as possible.

Bit by bit she got used to her totally new life,

and bit by bit began to feel truly independent. All that came to an end one day, however, when answering a knock at the door after Alice had departed for work.

Ten

*T*he FBI is not famous for failing to conclude any investigation they may have started. Answering the knock at the door after Alice had departed for work, Clarity found herself confronted by two well-dressed and polite young men who announced themselves as FBI special agents and showed badges to prove it.

"FBI, Miss Kaitland. Could we have a word with you?" And, "It would mostly be about events before the shooting."

Their presence had taken Clarity completely by surprise. The demands of work at *The Farmingdale Weekly News,* along with adjusting to a new life of being away from her family and on her own, had worn away much of the shock of the mass shooting. And if nothing else, Clarity had become used to officialdom in every way, with the FBI no exception. She had been interviewed by the agency several times, with agents endlessly questioning her about any and everything possible she might have seen or heard when the armed woman burst into the newsroom of *The Farmingdale Weekly News* and had begun at once to spray everything and everyone with a shower of death from an AR-15 hand-held machine gun.

"What did the woman look like? How long was she in the newsroom before she started shooting? Did you duck down, or wasn't there time to hide? Did you actually see her break through the counter? Did she go for Elsworth Barnes last of all?"

But events before the shooting? What events? She tried to remember her first days of work and couldn't. The shooting had obliterated almost everything else. The past seemed sometimes not even to have existed. So it would probably be something near to nothing she'd observed when first employed. *Bear with it, Clarity,* she thought. *It can't take long.*

"Oh, good morning. Yes, of course," she said, and prepared to answer whatever all over again.

The two men seemed pleasant enough as she led them into the kitchen and indicated they should sit around the kitchen table. "Only me here," she said. "You just caught me, actually. I don't start work until after Alice has gone. Coffee?"

She got the coffee machine going and said,

"You're lucky to have found me. I only moved a few weeks ago and didn't tell my family or anyone else where I was going. Coffee up in a moment," she added. "So shoot. What can I tell you that you probably must already know?"

Clarity was a picture of innocence, her dark jumble of curls framing a face bland of any expression except, possibly, a look of cooperating curiosity. In spite of her ghastly experience in witnessing the terrible slaughter in the newspaper's newsroom, her longtime general naïveté saw her through it all, first at home and jobless once more, and then again while the newspaper almost miraculously survived under the helm of the remarkably undaunted Roslind Bernstein.

Slowly isolating herself from most of her memories, Clarity had fitted almost effortlessly into her new role as a columnist. To her, it was as though all that had occurred had happened to someone else, leaving her to get on with ferreting about researching in the unknown, just as she always had her whole life, in school, at home, and then at *The Farmingdale Weekly News.*

She served the two pleasant FBI agents their coffee and sat back down at the table and waited for the agents' questioning to begin.

"Just a few words about the day you spent at Indian River," One of the FBI agents said. "Won't keep you long."

Indian River? That certainly came out of the blue, How did they know she'd gone there? She couldn't remember telling anybody. She'd even forgotten all about going there herself. But, yes, she'd got in her car and driven there one day, hadn't she, hoping to find something about the Women Warrior hate group whom she'd uncovered while hunched over her laptop staring at pictures of them in their website wearing Nazi storm trooper uniforms and giving Hitler-like Nazi salutes to their leader. Was it the Fourth of July? She closed her eyes, trying to remember, and couldn't, except it had been a waste of time and, preparing for whatever useless questions were still to come, she hardly heard one agent say, "Can you tell us why you went there?"

That was the younger of the two men, his pleasant smile as completely disarming as his impeccable grooming, his business suit and muted tie.

She could only stare blankly and in silence as the agent shot a stream of questions, one right after another, "When did you go there? In the morning or the afternoon?" and, "How long did you stay?"

After another moment's silence around the kitchen table, while the men waited with an implacable pleasantness for her to answer, Clarity finally stammered out an irrelevant answer. "I think it was the fourth. The newspaper was closed, and I think I remember wanting to look at the hate group there that I was researching."

Even as she spoke, some of the trip came back to her, and she remembered that she'd come away from Indian River with a bunch of Woman

Warrior pamphlets, and a beaten-up swastika flag she'd stuffed in her desk drawer, and then had taken home to show Alice. But for the life of her she couldn't remember how she'd got them, and she'd never seen a single one of the Warriors.

Eleven

Arriving at the small town amidst all the holiday celebrations, finding a place to park and wearing a hoodie, since she knew that from all the newspaper photos of her that she might be recognized, she'd asked a dozen people who either knew nothing or froze up at the mere mention of the Warriors. She'd looked here and there for signs of them and had seen none. The hateful Nazi women who endlessly spread online their deadly lies were like shadows, ghosts. You knew they were there but could never see them.

The first person she'd approached, she vaguely remembered, was a police officer she thought certainly must know about the hateful Women Warriors. He had stopped directing traffic to ticket a motorist he had just pulled over for blatantly running a red light, and the driver was angrily cursing him out and calling him a bloody pig. She couldn't remember more except some teenage girls giggling and laughing in the car's back seat.

The police officer had disappointingly failed to know anything at all about the hate group, and thinking they might have some sort of an encampment outside the town, she'd imagined a tent big enough to hold meetings in. Undaunted, she had driven around the barren outskirts of Indian River but disappointingly had seen nothing even remotely approaching an encampment.

Back in town, she'd mingled with the crowd watching the Fourth of July parade, featuring Indian River vets, and a memorial ceremony on the village green opposite its town hall, and was again disappointed not to see anyone resembling Nazis or even neo-Nazism. She saw no banners emblazoned with swastikas, no Storm Trooper types parading by in a group, heard no speeches filled with hateful words.

Her vague hazy jumble of memories were briefly interrupted again by the FBI agents. From one, "Miss Kaitland, when was the decision made to have you go to Indian River?" And from the other, "Which person gave you the order, and who did you meet?"

Order me? Meet someone? Clarity barely heard them What on earth were they talking about?

Her mind slipped back into remembering how,

in her frustration, she had turned to the one place and person she was certain would know, if anybody, where and how to find members of the women's hate group, and surprisingly she'd found the pharmacy open. A pleasant and talkative woman who chatted about the town, the pharmacist had suddenly become frozen in manner when Clarity, who had decided the way to get information was to pretend to be one of the Warriors and there to buy first aid items for the group, said casually, "They're for one of our Warrior group; She got scrapes in a bad fall."

The pharmacist's pleasant manner had instantly changed. She'd pulled the things away Clarity had asked for and which she'd placed on the counter and said, "You're one of that crowd? Get out of here, please." And had turned her back.

More rambling vague memories were interrupted by the older FBI agent, who, glancing at some notes, said, "Who did you see besides the pharmacist? And why her? She isn't a Nazi, nor a member of the Warriors."

And the younger one broke in to say, "We know your connection, Miss Kaitland. So who else? It's in your own interest to tell us now rather than later."

And, "If you can't help us here, then it will have to be in custody. "

They gave a suddenly surprised and bewildered Clarity little chance to think further. What they were up to came next with a complete change of manner. The politeness was suddenly gone. "Why don't you quit stalling around, Miss Kaitland," the older agent said.

"You're only making things more difficult for yourself in keeping silent," came from the other. "You're in for thirty years at least, Miss Kaitland. Talking now could lessen that."

And for the first time, Clarity, who had been so immersed in a blur of near forgotten memories as to think of nothing else, realized with sickening shock that she was thought to be one of the Women Warriors who'd stormed into the newsroom on that awful day to begin killing people.

Twelve

Roslind Bernstein was in Elsworth Barne's old office and on the phone to the newspaper's printer when Benny Cranz, limping badly and with one leg still bandaged and in a brace, burst in on her.

"Have you heard?" And then when she lowered the phone in surprise, he blurted out, "About Clarity. Tracy Tangerton just called in about it."

"Clarity? What about her?" Roslind had only read that morning, when first coming in, Clarity's latest op-ed. It was bristling with attacks on Tory Lundt, listing his many failures in business in which he had criminally, she'd written, defrauded suppliers.

Looking past Benny, Roslind saw that Clarity

was not yet there, and a thought flashed that she had been in an accident, replacing instant worry that she might have brought a lawsuit down on their heads.

Benny's reply that apparently Clarity had been arrested and was being held in custody by the FBI hit her like a stone. "She what?" she managed.

Benny repeated the news Tracy had phoned in.

"She's been arrested by the FBI."

"The FBI?" Roslind begam to recover her thoughts.

"Arrested? What the hell for?"

Benny took a deep breath. "Tracy said for being an accessory to the attack."

"An accessory? Clarity?" Roslind tried to picture Clarity as somehow being part of the slaughter. She couldn't. Not Clarity. She could only see her small scholarly face peeping out from behind her mass of black curls when hunched over the laptop.

"And for obstructing justice," Benny said, and added, "Apparently, Tracy says, they got her connected with some Nazi hate group called the Women Warriors over at Indian River because she made a visit there on July fourth, and because she was the one person here unscathed when the killer came in."

"It's not possible," Roslind breathed almost inaudibly. "Not Clarity." Her mind raced through all the times she remembered when, after the slaughter and while she was in the hospital, only half aware of all that was going on, of Clarity being headlined as a heroine who had miraculously survived.

She sat down numbly at her desk, and Benny Cranz waited along with everyone else in the gone-dead-silent newsroom for her to say something. She didn't. Not until she'd grabbed a phone, dialed a number, and barked at whomever answered. "It's Roslind Bernstein, the *Farmingdale Weekly*. Put Spencer Crown on, please."

A moment's silence and then the newsroom heard her say, "Spence? Roslind. Got a big case for you. And starting right now."

Spencer Crown, almost everyone in the newsroom knew, was a lawyer with the firm of Crown, Stacy and Boyd who was famous statewide for his relentless prosecuting manner that had landed numerous accused in jail. And as he answered the call and Roslind spoke to him, the newsroom heard words that everyone knew would be the paper's headlines for the next several issues at least.

"Spence, the goddamned feds have locked up one of mine at the newspaper. Clarity. Yeah, Clarity Kaitland. That's right. The one the President praised on a call. I'm sure you read her column this week on Lundt. Why was she arrested? I don't know the details, but apparently not for the Lundt article, but for some ridiculous fucking charge that she was an accessory to the gun slaughter here. Well, we're not having that nonsense. And you've got an innocent falsely accused woman on your hands, Spence."

And then, "Today. Right. I'll expect you." Roslind slammed the receiver back down and spun in her chair to face the still silent news room. Suddenly she was not the Roslind she'd been since the slaughter, a relatively quiet and reasonable boss who had seemed more human as she helped others get adjusted to being back on the job and to overcome what had happened to all their friends and colleagues. She was the tough Roslind of before the tragic shooting.

"Got all that? Yes?" Her tone said she'd dared anybody to object. "Well, don't just sit there gawking. Get busy. Bill, run up to Indian River and find out whatever you can. And don't ask me where to start. You're a reporter. Clarity went there on the Fourth of July and was apparently looking for the Women Warriors, so don't come back until you find out something, anything. Who did she contact, if anyone? And if she did, were they possibly connected to that Nazi bunch?"

"Brad, get onto Clarity's laptop on her desk. I'll want a printed copy of all her emails for the last three months, and pull up and print anything you can find in her ferreting about for whatever info she could get on the Nazi group. You know Clarity. She always had her head deep into finding out something or other, and it wasn't just bloody ancient Greeks."

Roslind broke off briefly and then said to Betsy Brine, "Betsy, get to the Kaitland family, and see what you can uncover there, if anything. Sean Kaitland is a surveyor for the county and also a firm supporter of Tory Lundt. Clarity's leaving home was partially due to that. See if the 'yellow-orange turd,' as she called Lundt, was possibly involved, or some of his followers and allies."

She turned to the two new reporters, Agnes Peril and Brian Noonan, who had both come from faraway papers to help their fellow reporters.

"Aggie, Brian," Roslind said. "Get busy looking into Alice somebody Clarity shared an apartment with and find out who Clarity had for friends, if any. She was pretty antisocial, but Alice wasn't, I understand, and she and Clarity were close. Who is Alice, anyway? How does she think politically, if at all? What about her family and friends?"

"And Randy," she said, addressing Randy Colefield, a writer who had been badly wounded but had, along with Roslind and Benny Cranz and Betsy Brine, miraculously survived, "Get onto Clarity's school background, her friends if she had any, her teachers. Were any of them neo-Nazis or white nationalists?"

It went like that all day and the day after. Roslind was merciless. "Our lawyer is the best," she said, "but he's not an investigator; we are. All of us. We're first and foremost as reporters just that. We scurry deep into news items we consider of interest to the public, and far too often buried or obscure, in order to dig out facts—the truth. Well, one of our number is in trouble. So get busy, damn it. Do just that and find out why and how it was impossible for Clarity of all people to have done what they accuse her of."

Thirteen

The windowless heavily barred isolation cell was eight feet by four feet with a cot, a seatless toilet, and a sink with a cold water tap. Lying on the cot, Clarity tried to make sense of all that had happened to her from the moment she had suddenly become aware that the two FBI agents suspected her of somehow being involved in the mass shooting at *The Farmingdale Weekly News.*

Their friendliness had abruptly disappeared when one of them had said, "Give up your nonsense, Miss Kaitland. You're only making things more difficult for yourself."

And the other saying, "We know you are part of the Women Warriors gang. So do everyone a favor, yourself included, and tell us just what part you played in the massacre."

And her own bewildered protests among them, her saying, "There wasn't any gang. Just one woman wearing a hood."

"What was her name, Miss Kaitland?" And, "Was she the gang leader?"

And then being handcuffed and walked out of the apartment she shared with Alice to a police station, and mugged, and then being locked up forever, until some big imposing and authoritative gray-haired man named Spencer Crown appeared, who said Roslind Bernstein had hired him as her lawyer, and had asked her to explain for the millionth time why she had gone to Indian River and what she had done there.

How desperately she had tried to explain to Spencer Crown that she had gone there only because she'd thought to find out more about the Women Warriors when she'd discovered them to be so nearby. "It was just on sudden impulse, Mr. Crown. *The Farmingdale Weekly* was closed for the Fourth of July, and I had nothing else to do."

"And just whom did you plan to see?"

"I didn't plan to see anybody. I just thought I'd get to see the Nazis in a parade if there was one. Like the white nationalists at Charlottesville."

He hadn't seemed really to have believed a word she said, except to say repeatedly, "We'll try to get around that."

And in between all his questions, there was his endlessly asking when she had first become interested in the Women Warriors, almost as though she had indeed been part of them, and making her defense seem a hopeless case.

For two days after he'd left, and as the hours endlessly ticked by, Clarity found herself staring at a tiny spider web high in a corner of the cell where one wall met the ceiling. The little spider shared the web with a fly that had become ensnared, at first struggling to free itself, then had remained motionless and quiet, never to move again. And Clarity felt herself like it, surrounded by an imprisonment from which there was no escape.

Twice she was taken to the visitor room, where she sat looking through a glass wall at first her mother, Angel, whose distress at her being there was mixed with anger and who could hardly bring herself to speak for tears.

"Do you realize, Clarity, what you've done? No you don't. You secretly got yourself involved with some Nazi bunch you heard about from that SPLC outfit or whatever they're called. Were you out of your mind?"

And, "Have you given one thought to what you have done to your family? The awful embarrassment for Abigail and Arlene at their jobs. To say nothing of me at mine. I can't meet the eye of any customer. And especially to your father, who could lose his job any day because of you. Dad won't allow anyone to even speak about you. He says you're dead. Period."

Her other visitor, whose unexpected appearance

came as a shock and at first frightened her, was Roslind Bernstein. The editor surprised her completely when she appeared on the other side of the glass wall wearing a pleasant smile. Why on earth was she there? Surely she must be angry, even betrayed, with *The Farmingdale Weekly News* written up in other newspapers all over and more often than not maligned.

"This is what you get with a lot of left-wing nonsense," said one editorial writer, echoing her father. Another one, clearly pro Lundt, headlined, "*Farmingdale Weekly,* a hot bed of godless anti-Americanism." And from another, prestigious nationwide paper, "*The Farmingdale Weekly News,* a small town local paper, puts honest journalism everywhere at risk."

"I don't want you to worry, Clarity," Roslind said, still smiling. "First, what can I bring you to make you more comfortable? You've only got a week more in here, but you poor thing, this cell is so cold and barren. A good warm throw, would that help?" And then, "Don't worry, dear girl. We're going to get you out of this. We're halfway there. But I need a little more information from you if possible."

And Roslind had asked her specifically, just as Crown had, but more intently, about the Nazi salute she'd given. And, "The Nazi flag the cops found in your desk drawer. Where did you get it from, for Heaven's sake, and when? And Clarity, we need to know exactly, if possible, what you might have said to the pharmacist when you were buying some things from her, and just what those things were?"

Clarity tried to remember. Her visit to Indian River on the Fourth seemed such a jumble now, of little vague patches of memory that came and went but seemed to mean so much to both her attorney and Roslind Bernstein. And above all, there was the one question that both Spencer Crown and Roslind seemed to insist on. They'd learned she visited some elderly bookstore owner. Why had she? And what had she and the man talked about?

Her answer, "We talked about Hitler and Mussolini and how they had risen to power before World War II."

"And what else?" Roslind had seemed slightly disbelieving.

The memory fog deepened in Clarity. She couldn't recall.

"Never mind," Roslind said. "We'll find out."

And then she was gone, and with her any hope Clarity had begun to feel when she'd first come. And the next days passed in a nightmare of police and officialdom, until she found herself before a judge and a jury, and her trial had begun.

Fourteen

"All rise."

The judge in the trial of the State v. Clarity Kaitland had appeared. He was a graying man with tired eyes and an authoritative air, in keeping with his years at the bench. He said, "Please all sit down," and the prosecution began its opening arguments.

The courtroom was packed with visitors and the press along with court officials. It was a cheerless drab room matching the lost lonely appearance of the defendant, who sat a huddled figure next to her attorney, Spencer Crown, trying not to hear the accusations thrown against her and awaiting for his words of defense on her behalf.

"The accused," the prosecutor leveled at the

silently waiting jury and pointing a stabbing finger at Clarity, "as we will show with cold facts, was a secretive member of the Women Warriors, a notorious Nazi hate group, and obstructed justice in the arrest of those guilty of an appalling assault that cost the lives of six innocent persons. Don't be dissuaded by her innocent appearance, a role she has chosen for years to hide her evil. She is a killer, as we will shortly prove."

Clarity barely heard. She had retreated as she had almost from the first day of her arrest into a kind of nonthinking numbness at everything thrown at her, living day by day leading to the implacable hostile atmosphere of the courtroom, to which she was brought in an orange prison suit, her hands manacled, until released to sit by her counsel by uniformed court police officers.

She heard, but didn't listen to, the accusations thrown at her by the prosecutor, a slight wiry man who sported a razor-thin mustache that abetted his ever-present air of sarcasm and disbelief whenever he mentioned her name. Nor did she hear him when he promised to summon witnesses to what he called her cold-blooded calumny.

Nor did she hear Spencer Crown, who rose to speak for her when it came to the turn of the defense to cross-examine, to say how he would dissemble every fact presented against her. Nor see the silent spectators behind her, one of her sisters, Abigail, and Alice, with whom she'd shared an apartment.

She sat numb the first day, barely hearing the prosecutor, thinking perhaps also of that day so very long ago now when she had shyly but angrily come to the newspaper to ask big frizzy-haired Geraldine Banner why she was getting no answers to her advertising in the paper's classifieds to her requests for a job. And had almost turned away, completely discouraged, until magically rescued by the sudden unexpected appearance of the venerable Elsworth Barnes.

The prosecutor called his first witness to her calumny to the witness box to condemn Clarity, then another and another. The jury heard of her own self-proclaimed membership in the Nazi hate group to a local pharmacist, and she had been proved of that membership in the discovery amidst her personal things at the home she shared with one Alice Salis of a Warrior pamphlet listing her among its members. With it was also found a Nazi swastika flag and Hitler's infamous *Mein Kampf.* They heard of an openly public Nazi salute she'd been seen giving, and throughout everything brought to bear by the prosecution, her being the one unhurt person in the newsroom slaughter, a passive observer to all of it from start to finish.

Even before the prosecutor had ended his litany of accusations labeling Clarity guilty beyond any reasonable doubt, a casual court observer would have noticed that the jury seemed to have already made up its mind. One after another, jury members had begun to look bored. Some even yawned, and one elderly man was seen nodding to sleep.

But the jury was premature in any judgment. The defense counsel, Spencer Crown, had waited patiently for the prosecution to finish its case before he began his own. As he had approached to cross-examine the last witness in the box to condemn his client, perhaps at least one juror was surprised to see him catch the eye of Roslind Bernstein, who throughout all the prosecution's parade of guilty evidence had sat taking in every damning accusation with an air of quiet confidence.

A short silent look passed between Spencer Crown and her, and then, after a court recess, it was the turn of the defense, and Spencer went to work.

Fifteen

An undaunted defender, when he took the offensive, Spencer first brought on a surprise witness. This was a man named Ralph Parker, a stocky person with a neatly trimmed beard and carefully combed short hair, who identified himself as was one of the town of Indian River police officers.

"I'll keep this short, Officer Parker," the imposing defense attorney said. "You heard testimony from pharmacist Marjorie Ditotter. Can you explain her statement that the defendant was, in her own words, a member of the notorious Nazi Women Warriors?"

The firmly confident police office responded immediately. "Sure," he said. "The defendant said she was a member of the Women Warriors because I told her to say so."

There was an audible sudden movement among the jurors, as though they had been awakened.

"Could you kindly explain, Officer Parker?"

"Sure. I was directing traffic on the Fourth, and that lady there," he nodded at Clarity, "came up to me and said she was a reporter for *The Farmingdale Weekly News* and a stranger to Indian River, and could I suggest where she could begin to unearth information about the women Nazi bunch, perhaps even get to meet one, since her research said they were headquartered in my town."

"And?" Crown prompted mildly.

"And I told her," the officer continued, "that her best bet would be to pretend she was one in hope, maybe, that she'd hit on one who actually was. We're a small town, and unfortunately, they seem to be all over the place. Saying you are one seemed to me the best way to unearth one since they are a cult in which they all stick together."

"And?"

"And she thanked me, and I remember her laughing and saying, 'Then I'll have to get in practice,' or something like that, right? and her tossing up a quick Nazi salute. And I laughed and said it was perfect and threw a salute myself right back at her."

There was an even greater stir in the jury. Spencer Crown thanked Officer Parker, and called a Carolyn Winder to the stand. She was a young, trim, neatly dressed woman with long blond hair and an air of quiet authority beyond her years who identified herself when asked and said she was the librarian at the town's small public library.

"You visited the Good Rx Pharmacy on the Fourth?" And when she answered in the affirmative, Crown asked her if she had met the defendant there, and what had passed between them.

"I came in," she replied, "just as the pharmacist was telling her to get out of the store because she wasn't serving any damned Nazi woman. And I remember I was surprised because I thought I remembered seeing her at the library when she asked me for a book on Greek history. I simply was astonished, frankly, to hear her say she was a Warrior member."

"And?"

"Well, there was one way to tell. I see everything in Indian River in my job as librarian, and I know a lot about those awful women and the hate they spread. They are all tattooed with a Nazi swastikas, on the back of their hands or wrists, and sometimes all over their bodies."

"And?"

"Well, on the way out, I impulsively stopped her and said, 'You're not a Nazi. You're a reporter with *The Farmingdale Weekly News.* So why are you pretending to be one?' And she said that a police officer had suggested she do so. I looked at the back of both her hands and her wrists and saw no tattoos. So, if she actually is a Nazi, I'm Taylor Swift."

The courtroom burst into laughter. Even the judge allowed himself a smile.

Crown next called an elderly bookstore owner. After he'd identified himself, Crown attacked more of the prosecution's vital evidence of Clarity's guilt and asked his witness if he'd had a visit from the defendant. The bookstore owner brightened visibly. "Oh, my, yes," he said, "and a most delightful one. I told her what I knew about the Women Warriors, and we talked then about their Nazi hero, Adolf Hitler, whom they sought to emulate. I gave Miss Kaitland an old copy I had of *Mein Kampf* I couldn't sell, and before she left, a tattered old swastika flag I'd picked up off the street, which had been dropped by one of them the last time they paraded."

The jury, now wide awake, quickly learned there was more proof of Clarity's innocence to come when Spencer Crown called his next witness to the stand, a tired looking man wearing spectacles who ran the town's small printing firm.

Crown waved the damning pamphlet that listed Clarity as a member of the Nazi group. "Did you print this?"

"Yes, my firm did," the printer said. "They had her listed as a member without asking her, and planned to demand money, like with some others they'd listed, if she wanted it out."

"I see. Blackmail. And you?" Crown demanded.

"They threatened my wife and my grandchildren if I didn't comply."

The murmurs grew throughout the courtroom. The jury now sat noticeably erect, and the judge, looking authoritatively severe, pounded his gavel for silence.

Spencer Crown dismissed the printer. A quick glance passed between him and Roslind Bernstein, and he called to the stand his next witness, Alice Salis, who identified herself as sharing an apartment with the defendant.

Crown wasted no time. "Miss Salis. I believe you found a leather jacket belonging to the defendant. It was something that apparently Forensics missed in visiting the home you share with her. Can you tell what you saw or found?"

"Well, it was where the defendant usually puts it when home from work. It was in the coatrack in the entrance hall the day after the shooting, and it was half off its hanger. When I went to hang it straight I saw a suspicious tear in its shoulder."

"Why suspicious?"

"Well, that wasn't at all like Clarity. She must have been too upset to notice. And she would never not have had it repaired if possible. She's very fastidious."

"And?"

"The leather goods shop, where I took it in hopes that it could be repaired, said I should take it to the police because they found a second tear in the jacket, a hole actually, and said both looked like bullet holes."

"Thank you, Miss Salis. You may step down."

In the dead hush that had fallen over the court-room and the jury, Crown then called a woman named Mary-Ann Terinovsky, who was quickly identified as a private forensics expert whose long and respected record in criminal cases of homicide was well known.

Enjoying her chance to be publicly import-ant, and speaking with unchallenged authority, the heavyset older woman said that both holes were indeed made by bullets, and in her judgment from a nine-millimeter bullet, similar to those used in the AR-15 that had been identified as the weapon used by the killer in the slaughter of newsroom staff.

"And similar to any other evidence of a shot, Miss Terinovsky?"

"Yes, sir. Leather strands of one bullet on the jacket matched some tiny wood tearings I found on a long, almost microscopic scratch on the surface of the desk in the defendant's alcove in the newsroom. While it was virtually invisible to the naked eye, under the microscope it proved to be caused by a bullet's trajectory."

"Meaning?'

"Meaning the defendant, Miss Kaitland, was among all those others shot at, and was miracu-lously lucky to have escaped the hail of bullets her-self."

The courtroom came near to erupting with a sudden outburst of clapping and several loud cheers. The judge severely called for order and pounded his gavel. The prosecutor and the counsel for the defense rose in turn to give their closing arguments, and the judge ordered the jury to retire to deliberate the innocence or guilt of the defendant. When they returned with an innocent verdict in less than thirty minutes, he dismissed the case, and told Clarity she was free to go.

Sixteen

Unobserved, the judge, after dismissing the case and in leaving the bench and the courtroom, had a quiet word with one of the court's uniformed police officers. The officer received instructions to ask Miss Kaitland if she could kindly come alone to his office before she left court.

Dutifully, the officer obeyed, and a surprised Clarity, only beginning to emerge from the nightmare of accusations that had threatened her with a life in prison, allowed herself to be escorted away from her more than happy defense counsel and from her editor-in-chief at *The Farmingdale Weekly News,* whom her attorney told her was the source of all the evidence he had brought to court in her defense.

"You had investigative reporting to thank for your freedom, Miss Kailand, not me," Spencer Crown told her firmly.

When the officer dutifully showed Clarity into the judge's inner chambers, she found herself in a silent paneled office with the judge who, without his black robes and seat above the court, was completely changed in appearance from a judicious high member of the law to an ordinary, rather studious-looking older man.

He looked up from his laptop the moment she entered. "Ah, Miss Kaitland," he said. "Thank you for coming in, and congratulations on your legal victory. I trust you are already savoring it."

And when Clarity, not knowing what to expect, mumbled, "Thank you," or some other useless words, and just stood and stared, he said, "Do sit down, won't you?" And rising from behind his desk, he indicated a chair, saying, "This should perhaps only take a few minutes."

Returned to his own seat, there was a long and what seemed an almost embarrassed silence on his part, and with Clarity not just wondering but totally aghast at finding herself alone with the judge, who for days had seemed more than anyone as though a god, with all possible power over her entire future.

But finally, and after what seemed an awkward forever, and with the judge embarrassedly clearing his throat, he said, "Miss Kaitland, I understand you are an ardent student of the early Greek bards, those near immortals who lightened life with their music and poetry after the Mycenean period of ancient Greece, around 1150 BC, I believe, when Greece fragmented into the many different Greek tribes and cities before the Homeric period of the Trojan War.

"I would so love, Miss Kaitland, to share our mutual knowledge and learn how far you had got in your studies before this recent unfortunate interruption in both our lives and our return to the ordinary."

End

About the Author

Author David Osborn, in a seventy-year career, has written over twenty feature motion pictures that include an Academy Award nomination, three three-act television plays, two ninety-minute two-hour documentaries, a memoir, and twenty novels. He lives in Connecticut with his wife, Robin, a once ballerina and then an icon in international health policy. Their daughter is a PhD clinical psychologist, and their son a distinguished lawyer representing animal rights worldwide.

Also by David Osborn

Novels and Screenwriting

Novels

The Glass Tower – Hodder & Stoughton
Open Season – The Dial Press
The French Decision – Doubleday
Love and Treason – New American Library
Heads – Bantam
Murder on Martha's Vineyard – Lynx
Murder on the Chesapeake – Simon & Schuster
Murder in the Napa Valley – Simon & Schuster
The Last Pope – Source Books
The Cape Cod Blue – Dagmar Miura
Alicia's Secret (young adult) – Dagmar Miura
A Cold Wind from the Andes – Dagmar Miura
The Head Hunters – Dagmar Miura
Looking Back: The Long Life of a Writer (a memoir)
Delta Red – Dagmar Miura
Eventide – Dagmar Miura
The Somersville Bodies – Dagmar Miura
Cold Case 369 – Dagmar Miura

The Lighthouse (a novella)– Dagmar Miura

The Saugatuck Conspiracy – Dagmar Miura

Bones – Dagmar Miura

Kira and Cassandra – Dagmar Miura

The Newsroom (a novella) – Dagmar Miura

For Children

Jessica and the Crocodile Knight (a novel) – HarperCollins

Jessica and Her Adventures in Fairyland (collection of five novellas) – Dagmar Miura

Ophelia and Her Forest Friends (series of ten stories) – Dagmar Miura

Jessica and the Witch's Broom – Dagmar Miura

Jessica and the Flying Unicorns – Dagmar Miura

Jessica and the Golden Swan Feather – Dagmar Miura

Feature Films

The Trap (original story and screenplay; Academy Award nominee for Best Foreign Film) – Columbia

Open Season (screenplay, adapted from Osborn's own best-selling novel *Open Season*) – Columbia

Chase a Crooked Shadow (original story and screenplay co-written with Charles Sinclair; listed by the British Academy of Motion Picture Science as "One of the ten best suspense scripts ever written") – Warner Bros.

Moment of Danger, a.k.a. *Malaga* (screenplay adapted from the novel) – Warner Bros.

Malaga (screenplay) – Warner Bros.

Maroc 7 (original story and screenplay) – J. Arthur Rank

Deadlier Than the Male (original story and screenplay) – J. Arthur Rank

Some Girls Do (original story and screenplay) – J. Arthur Rank

The Road to Dusty Death (screenplay) – J. Arthur Rank

The Games (screenplay) – Associated British

Follow the Boys (original story and screenplay) – MGM

Beat Girl (original story and screenplay) – Renown Films/British Lion

Stop-over Forever (original story and screenplay) – British Lion

Winter Holiday (original story and screenplay) – MGM

Penny Gold (original story and screenplay) – J. Arthur Rank/Columbia

Whoever Slew Auntie Roo? (original story and screenplay) – Paramount & American International

Murder, She Said (screenplay, Agatha Christie adaptation) – MGM

Murder at the Gallop (screenplay, Agatha Christie adaptation) – MGM

Feature-Length Documentaries

Fangio, The History of Formula One Racing (original
screenplay; executive producer) – Volpi
Productions

Why Ireland – Irish Tourist Bureau

Films Canceled While in Production

HMS Ulysses – Volpi Productions (screenplay
adaptation of the Alistair MacLean novel about
protecting North Sea convoys to Russia during
World War II; production halted when a key
warship was unavailable)

The Mad Motorists – Volpi Productions (screenplay
adaptation from the Allen Andrews novel about
the 1907 Peking to Paris race)

Eagle at Sundown – Dragon Films (original screen
story about Napoleon's escape from Elba;
starring Douglas Fairbanks; in production when
canceled)

Les Petits Rats – Disney (original story and
screenplay about the Paris Ballet school;
production begun, then canceled)

Hunters' Horn – McCahon Productions (screenplay
adaptation from the Harriette Simpson Arnow
novel; production canceled; financing failure)

Blood on the Rose – British Lion (screenplay
adaptation from the Phyllis Hastings novel)

Television

Bouquet for Miss Olive (three-act play; British Television Producers Association nominee for Best Play of the Year) – Granada/ITV

Three on a Gas Ring (three-act play; British Television Producers Association nominee for Best Play of the Year) – Granada/ITV

Why George Brown Hanged (three-act play) – Granada/ITV

Arthur of the Britons (pilot and three scripts on the life of King Arthur; Writers Guild of Great Britain award winner for Best British Children's Series)

The Antiquers (original story, pilot, and six episodes in the sitcom series) – Irish National Television

www.ingramcontent.com/pod-product-compliance
Lightning Source LLC
Chambersburg PA
CBHW040836010826
48978CB00012BB/777